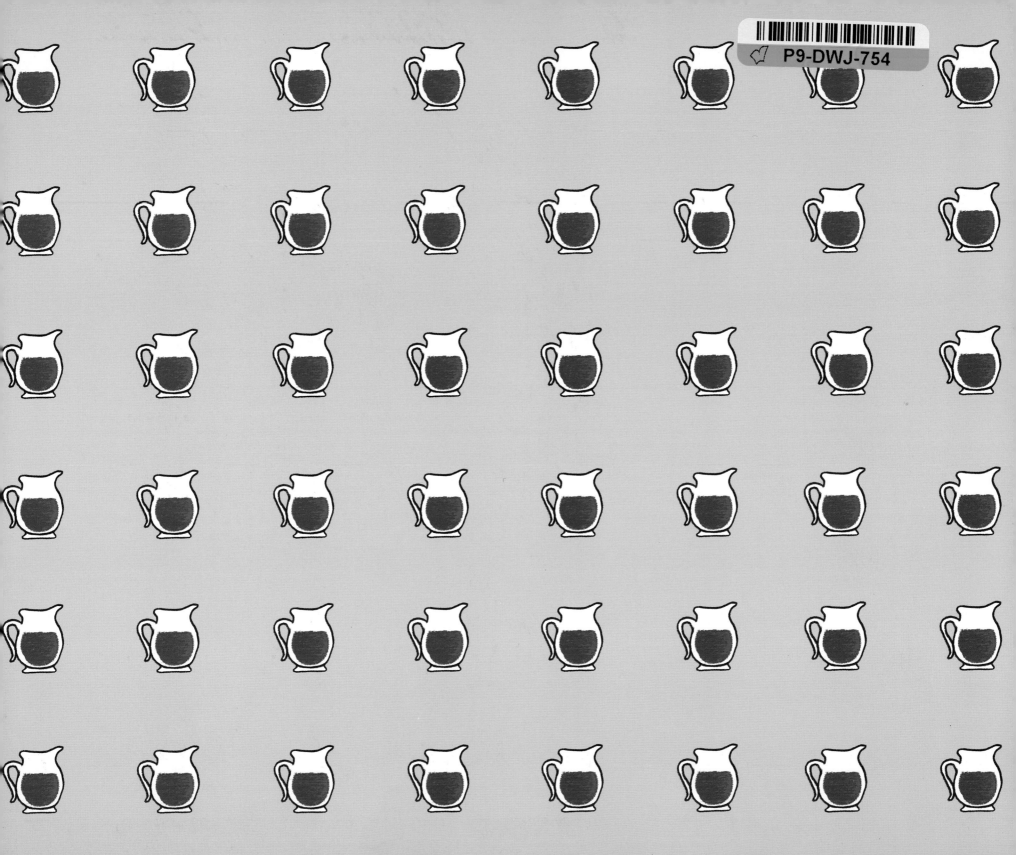

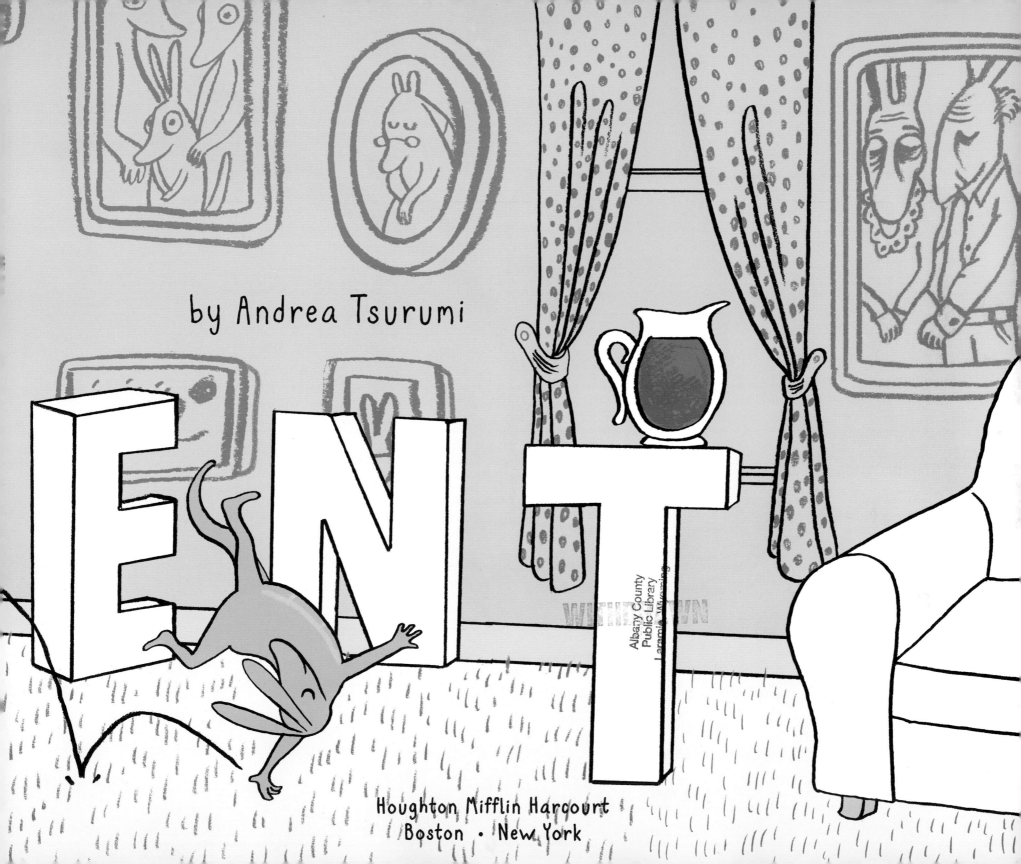

To Nina Frenkel,
brave chicken and
beloved friend

&

To Stephen Barr,
who made this
story possible

So Lola ran away from her mess and right into everyone else's.

Then Lola left everyone else's mess, and went back to her own.

The illustrations in this book were done using
graphite on Bristol vellum and digital color.
The text type was set in Andrea Tsurumi's handwriting.
The display type was hand-lettered by Andrea Tsurumi.

Library of Congress Cataloging-in-Publication Data is on file.

ISBN 978-0-544-94480-0

Manufactured in China
SCP 10 9 8 7 6 5 4 3 2 1
4500659632